Marianna May
and Nursey

Tomie dePaola

SIMON & SCHUSTER
BOOKS FOR YOUNG READERS
New York London Toronto Sydney New Delhi

For Tammy Grimes

SIMON & SCHUSTER BOOKS FOR YOUNG READERS
An imprint of Simon & Schuster Children's Publishing Division
1230 Avenue of the Americas, New York, New York 10020
Copyright © 1983 by Tomie dePaola
SIMON & SCHUSTER BOOKS FOR YOUNG READERS is a trademark of Simon & Schuster, Inc.
For information about special discounts for bulk purchases, please contact Simon & Schuster Special Sales
at 1-866-506-1949 or business@simonandschuster.com.
The Simon & Schuster Speakers Bureau can bring authors to your live event. For more information or to book an event,
contact the Simon & Schuster Speakers Bureau at 1-866-248-3049 or visit our website at www.simonspeakers.com.
Book design by Laurent Linn
The text for this book was set in Cantoria MT Std.
The illustrations for this book were rendered in acrylics on 150-pound Fabriano paper and enhanced with liquid dyes.
Manufactured in China
0320 SCP
First Edition
2 4 6 8 10 9 7 5 3 1
CIP data for this book is available from the Library of Congress.
ISBN 978-1-5344-6646-3
ISBN 978-1-5344-6647-0 (eBook)

Marianna May was *very* rich.
So were Papa and Mama.

Papa and Mama were *always* very busy.
So Marianna May had a lady who took care of her.
The lady's name was Nursey.

Nursey *always* wore white, white, white.
And so did Marianna May. Especially in summer.

Nursey didn't like it

when Marianna May rolled in the grass,

made mud pies,

ate orange ice

or strawberry ice cream.

Nursey didn't like it

when Marianna May painted pictures.

"Marianna May," said Nursey,
"sit nicely on the porch swing
and keep your white dress clean."

Even though Marianna May was very rich,
she was also very sad.

She liked rolling in the grass.

She liked making mud pies.

She liked orange ice and strawberry ice cream.

And she liked to paint pictures.

Mr. Talbot, who delivered the ice,
saw Marianna May sitting on the
porch swing day after day.
"How come you're always sittin', Missy?"
Mr. Talbot asked.

"Oh, Mr. Iceman, Nursey doesn't like it
if I get my dress all dirty. She doesn't like it
when I roll in the grass, or make mud pies,
or eat orange ice and strawberry ice cream.
And she especially doesn't like it
when I paint pictures."

"Aw, poor Missy," said Mr. Talbot,
and he took the ice around back.

"Poor little Missy doesn't look like
she's having much fun this summer, Aggie,"
Mr. Talbot said to the cook's helper.

"Poor Miss Marianna May isn't having much fun,"
Aggie said to Jack the cook.

"Minnie," said Jack to Nursey
(because that was Nursey's first name).
"Minnie, our little darlin' isn't having fun."

"Oh dear, Jack," said Nursey.
"Whatever shall we do?
Every time she plays, her dresses get all dirty."

"And they are very hard to get sparkling,"
said Mrs. Jones, who did the laundry.

Nursey, Mrs. Jones, Jack the cook,
Aggie, and Mr. Talbot all sat
down and gazed out the window.

Outside on the clothesline
hung Marianna May's white dresses.

"I have it," said Mr. Talbot, jumping up.

He told everyone his idea.

The next day, when Aggie
came back from the grocery store,
Jack put big kettles of water on the stove.
Mrs. Jones got out all the laundry tubs, and
Nursey rolled up her sleeves.

They worked all afternoon.

For the rest of the summer,
Marianna May rolled in the grass.

She made mud pies.

She ate orange ice.

She ate strawberry ice cream.

And she painted pictures.

for Mrs. Jones

for Jack

for Aggie

for mr. Talbot

for Nursey

for Papa and Mama

From that day on, there was only one time
when Marianna May wore white.